DISNEY · PIXAR

Toy to Toy

By Tennant Redbank

Illustrated by
Caroline Egan, Adrienne Brown,
Scott Tilley, and Studio IBOIX

Random House New York

These are Andy's toys.

Dear Parent:

Congratulations! Your child is taking the first steps on an exciting journey. The destination? Independent reading!

STEP INTO READING® will help your child get there. The program offers five steps to reading success. Each step includes fun stories and colorful art. There are also Step into Reading Sticker Books, Step into Reading Math Readers, Step into Reading Phonics Readers, Step into Reading Write-In Readers, and Step into Reading Phonics Boxed Sets—a complete literacy program with something to interest every child.

Learning to Read, Step by Step!

Ready to Read Preschool–Kindergarten
• big type and easy words • rhyme and rhythm • picture clues
For children who know the alphabet and are eager to begin reading.

Reading with Help Preschool–Grade 1
• basic vocabulary • short sentences • simple stories
For children who recognize familiar words and sound out new words with help.

Reading on Your Own Grades 1–3
• engaging characters • easy-to-follow plots • popular topics
For children who are ready to read on their own.

Reading Paragraphs Grades 2–3
• challenging vocabulary • short paragraphs • exciting stories
For newly independent readers who read simple sentences with confidence.

Ready for Chapters Grades 2–4
• chapters • longer paragraphs • full-color art
For children who want to take the plunge into chapter books but still like colorful pictures.

STEP INTO READING® is designed to give every child a successful reading experience. The grade levels are only guides. Children can progress through the steps at their own speed, developing confidence in their reading, no matter what their grade.

Remember, a lifetime love of reading starts with a single step!

Copyright © 2010 Disney/Pixar. All rights reserved.
Slinky® Dog is a registered trademark of Poof-Slinky, Inc. © Poof-Slinky, Inc.
Mr. Potato Head® and Tinkertoys® are registered trademarks of Hasbro, Inc. Used
with permission. © Hasbro, Inc. All rights reserved. Published in the United States
by Random House Children's Books, a division of Random House, Inc.,
1745 Broadway, New York, NY 10019, and in Canada by Random House of
Canada Limited, Toronto, in conjunction with Disney Enterprises, Inc.

Step into Reading, Random House, and the Random House colophon are registered
trademarks of Random House, Inc.

Visit us on the Web!
www.stepintoreading.com
www.randomhouse.com/kids

Educators and librarians, for a variety of teaching tools, visit us at
www.randomhouse.com/teachers

Library of Congress Cataloging-in-Publication Data
Redbank, Tennant.
Toy to toy / by Tennant Redbank ; illustrated by the Disney Storybook Artists.
p. cm. — (Step into reading. Step 1)
"Toy story 3."
ISBN 978-0-7364-2665-7 (trade) — ISBN 978-0-7364-8078-9 (lib. bdg.)
I. Disney Storybook Artists. II. Toy story 3 (Motion picture). III. Title.
PZ7.R24455To 2010 [E]—dc22 2009034874

Printed in the United States of America

10 9 8 7 6

Woody is a cowboy.

He wears a cowboy hat.

Buzz is a spaceman and
Woody's best friend.

Slinky is a dog.

He can stretch!

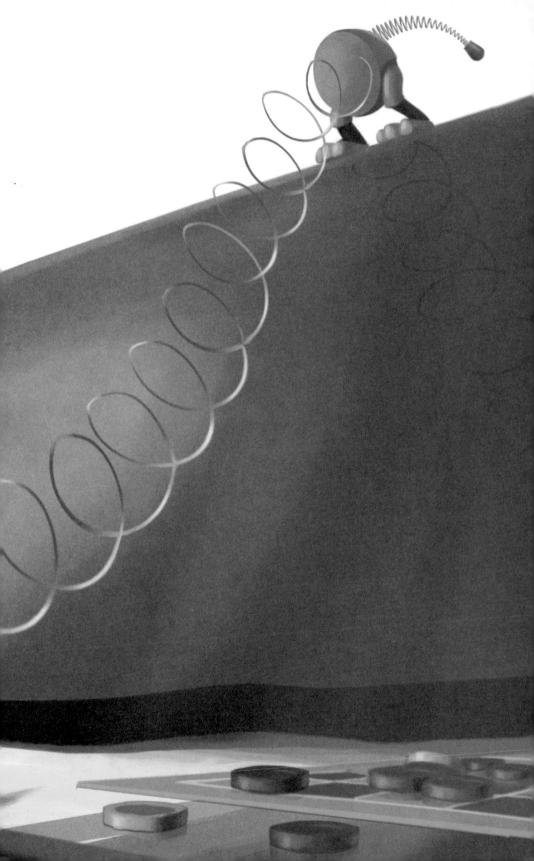

Yee-haw!

Jessie is a cowgirl.

She likes

to ride Bullseye.

Hamm is a piggy bank.

He holds pennies.

These toys are green.

They stick together.

Roar!

Rex is a dinosaur.

Andy is big now.

Andy's toys get
a new home.

They meet new toys!

Lotso is a teddy bear.

He is the boss.

Lotso likes to hug!

Big Baby is
the biggest toy.

Chunk has two faces.

Sparks spits
real sparks.

Twitch looks like

a big bad bug.

Stretch is made
of rubber.

All the toys
are ready to play!

Will Andy's toys like their new home?